Tess of the d'Urbervilles

by Thomas Hardy

CHAPTER ONE

A Noble Family

One evening, on his way home from Shaston to the village of Marlott, Jack Durbeyfield met Parson Tringham. 'Good evening, parson,' said Jack.

'Good evening, Sir John.'

Jack looked at the parson in surprise. 'Why do you call me "Sir John"?' he asked. 'You know that I am plain Jack Durbeyfield, the haggler.'

The parson hesitated for a moment, then replied, 'While I was researching the history of this county, I discovered that your ancestors are the d'Urbervilles, an ancient noble family. Your ancestor Sir Pagan d'Urberville was a famous knight who came from Normandy with William the Conqueror.'

'I have never heard it before!'

'Yes. Yours is one of the best families in England.'

'How amazing!' cried Jack. 'All these years I thought I was just a common fellow! Tell me, sir, where do we d'Urbervilles live?'

'You don't live anywhere. You are extinct as a county family.'

'That's bad. But where are we buried?'

'At Kingsbere. Many d'Urbervilles are buried there in marble tombs.'

'And where are our fine houses and our lands?'

'You don't have any, though you once had. Goodnight, Durbeyfield.'

'Well!' thought Jack. 'I'll go to The Pure Drop Pub and have a drink to celebrate this! Then I'll ride home in a carriage!'

That evening the women of the village were walking in a procession. It was an old custom. Every year, in the month of May, the women dressed in white and walked together through the village then danced in the field. As they passed by The Pure Drop Pub, one girl called out to another, 'Look, Tess Durbeyfield! There's your father riding home in a carriage!'

Tess turned to look. She was very pretty, with a soft mouth and large innocent eyes. She wore a white muslin dress and a red ribbon in her hair. None of the other girls had a red ribbon.

'Tess!' called her father from the carriage, 'I am descended from a noble family! I have a family vault at Kingsbere!'

Tess blushed to see her father make such a fool of himself. 'He's just tired,' she said.

'No!' said the other girl. 'He's drunk!'

'I won't walk with you if you make fun of my father!' cried Tess.

As the carriage drove away, the procession of women entered the field and began to dance.

Three young gentlemen were passing at that moment. They stopped to watch the women dancing. The youngest entered the field.

'What are you doing, Angel?' asked his eldest brother.

'I'm going to dance with them. Why don't we all dance?'

'Don't be foolish. We can't dance with simple country girls. Somebody might see us. Besides, we must get to Stourcastle before dark.'

'Well, you go on. I'll join you in five minutes.'

The two elder brothers - Felix and Cuthbert - walked on.

'Who will dance with me?' Angel asked the women.

'You'll have to choose a partner, sir,' said one of the girls.

Angel looked around and chose the girl nearest to him. He did not choose Tess, even though she was descended from a noble family.

After the dance, Angel noticed Tess. She was standing apart from the others, looking at him sadly. He felt sorry that he had not asked her to dance, but it was too late now. Angel turned and ran down the road after his brothers.

When Tess returned home that evening, she was still thinking about the young man who had not asked her to dance. But as soon as she entered the cottage, her father told her what the parson had said. 'I went back to The Pure Drop and told everyone there. One man said there is a lady called Mrs Stoke-d'Urberville living in a fine house near Trantridge. She must be my cousin.'

Mrs Durbeyfield smiled. Her face still had some of the freshness and prettiness of her youth. Tess's good looks came from her mother, not from the noble d'Urbervilles. 'I think you should go and visit her, Tess!' said she. 'I looked in my fortune-telling book and it said you should go!' Tess's mother was a simple country woman who spoke in dialect, sang folk songs, and had many superstitious beliefs. Tess had been educated at the National School and she spoke two languages: dialect at home, and English outside.

Mr and Mrs Durbeyfield had brought nine children into the world. Tess, the eldest, was seventeen. The two after Tess had died in infancy. Then came Liza-Lu, Abraham, two more sisters, a three-year-old boy, and the baby.

Mr Durbeyfield's face was red from drinking. 'I'm tired, Joan,' he said to his wife.

'Father,' said Tess, 'you have to drive the goods to town so we can sell them at the market tomorrow! How will you wake up in time?'

'I'll wake up, don't you worry!' said Jack.

But at two in the morning Joan came to Tess's room. 'I've been trying to wake him, but I can't,' she said. 'If he doesn't leave now, he'll be late for the market!'

'Abraham and I will go,' Tess replied.

Tess loaded the goods onto the cart, which was drawn by Prince, their only horse. Then she and Abraham climbed on and waved goodbye to their mother.

The night sky was full of stars as Tess and Abraham rode along.

'What do you think the stars are?' asked Abraham.

'They are worlds like this one.'

'Really? Are they exactly like our world?'

'No. I think they are like the apples on the tree. Some of them are splendid and healthy but others are rotten.'

'And which are we on - a splendid one or a rotten one?'

'A rotten one.'

They stopped talking, and Tess began to feel sleepy. She tried to stay awake, but in the end she fell asleep. She was woken up by the terrifying sound of an animal in pain. The cart had stopped.

Tess jumped down and saw to her horror that they had crashed into the morning mail-cart in the dark. The pointed wooden shaft of the mail-cart had penetrated Prince's chest like a sword. Tess put her hand on the wound. Prince's blood splashed over her face and dress. The poor horse fell down dead.

'I must go on with the mail,' said the mail-man. 'I'll send someone to help you.'

As Tess and Abraham waited on the road, the sun rose. Then Tess saw the huge pool of blood. 'It's all my fault!' she cried.

'How will mother and father get their goods to market without a horse?'

'Is it because we live on a rotten star?' asked Abraham, with tears running down his cheeks. Tess did not reply. Her cheeks were pale and dry, as though she thought herself a murderess.

After Prince's death, life was very difficult for the Durbeyfields. Tess felt responsible for her family's distress and wondered what she could do to help them. One day her mother said, 'Tess, you must go to our cousin Mrs Stoke-d'Urberville and ask for her help. She is very rich.'

Tess took a cart to Trantridge Cross and walked the rest of the way. She passed through The Chase, an ancient forest that had been there for thousands of years. Finally she came to Mrs d'Urberville's house, a fine new mansion known as The Slopes.

Tess was startled and intimidated by the grandeur of The Slopes. The great red-brick house, the green lawn with an ornamental tent on it, the stables: everything about the house and gardens looked like money. 'I thought we were an old family!' thought Tess, 'but this is all new!'

In fact the Stoke-d'Urbervilles were not really d'Urbervilles at all. Mr Simon Stoke had made a fortune as a merchant in the North of England. When he retired, he moved to the South and decided to change his name to something more aristocratic. He looked through a history of the county and found the name d'Urberville. So he changed his name to Stoke-d'Urberville. Tess and her family knew nothing about this work of the imagination.

As Tess stood looking at the house, a young man walked out of the ornamental tent, smoking a cigar. He had dark skin, a full mouth, and a black moustache. 'Well, my beauty, what can I do for you?' he asked, looking at Tess coldly. 'I am Mr Alexander d'Urberville. Have you come to see me or my mother?'

Tess was even more surprised by Mr d'Urberville than she was by the house. She had expected her cousins to have fine aristocratic faces, but this man looked almost barbaric.

'I've come to see your mother, sir,' she said.

'You can't see my mother: she is an invalid. Can I help you? What did you wish to discuss with her?'

Tess felt suddenly embarrassed. 'It's so foolish,' she said, smiling shyly. 'I'm afraid to tell you.'

'I like foolish things.'

'I came to tell you that we're of the same family as you.'

'Poor relations?'

'Yes.'

'Stokes?'

'No, d'Urbervilles.'

'Oh, yes. I mean d'Urbervilles.'

'Our name is now Durbeyfield, but we have proof that we are d'Urbervilles. We have an old seal, marked with a lion rampant. And we have an old silver spoon with a castle on it, but it is so worn that mother uses it to stir the soup.'

'A castle argent is certainly my crest,' said he. 'And my arms a lion rampant. And so, you have come on a friendly visit to us, as relations?'

'Yes,' said Tess, looking up again. 'I will go home by the same cart that brought me.'

'The cart won't come for a long time yet. Why not walk with me around the grounds, my pretty cousin?'

Tess wished she could leave immediately, but the young man insisted, so she walked around the grounds with him. He showed her gardens, fruit trees, and greenhouses. In one of the greenhouses, he asked Tess if she liked strawberries.

'Yes,' she replied, 'when they are in season.'

'They are in season here already,' said Alec. He picked a ripe red strawberry and held it to her lips.

'No - no!' she said quickly, putting her fingers between his hand and her lips. 'Please let me take it in my own hand.'

'Nonsense!' he insisted. A little distressed, she parted her lips and took it in.

Alec asked her many questions about herself and her family. She told him about the death of Prince. 'It was all my fault!' she said. 'And now we are even poorer than we were before.'

'Maybe I can do something to help,' said Alec. 'My mother could find work for you here. But if you come to live here, Tess, you mustn't talk nonsense about being a d'Urberville. Your name is Durbeyfield - a completely different name.'

'I wish for no better name, sir,' said Tess with dignity.

CHAPTER TWO

Maiden

Then Tess got home the next day, her mother said, 'A letter has come, Tess! Mrs d'Urberville wants you to work on her chicken farm. She says you will have a comfortable room and good wages!'

Tess read the letter, then said, 'I want to stay here with you and father.'

'Why?'

'I don't want to tell you why. I don't really know why.' For the next few weeks, Tess searched for work close to home, but she found none. One day, when she came home, her mother said, 'Mr d'Urberville came by on his horse and asked if you had decided to work at his mother's chicken farm. Oh, what a handsome man he is!'

'I don't think so,' said Tess coldly.

'And he was wearing a diamond ring!' said Abraham. 'I saw it. The diamond glittered every time he put his hand up to his moustache. Why did our rich relation put his hand up to his moustache so often?'

'Perhaps to show his diamond ring,' said Jack.

'Are you going to accept the offer, Tess?' asked her mother.

'Perhaps,' said Tess.

'Well, he likes her,' said Joan to her husband, 'and she should go.'

'I don't like my children going away from home,' said Jack.

'Let her go,' said his poor stupid wife. 'He likes her, and he called her "cousin"! Maybe he'll marry her, and then we will have a new horse and plenty of money!'

'I will go,' said Tess. 'But don't talk about me marrying him. I am going to earn some money so that we can buy a horse.'

Tess wrote to Mrs d'Urberville, accepting her offer. Mrs d'Urberville replied, saying she was glad. Mrs d'Urberville's handwriting seemed rather masculine.

Two days later, the entire family accompanied Tess to meet the cart. As they climbed the hill, the cart appeared on the summit. Tess kissed everyone goodbye and ran up the hill. But then a gig came out from behind the trees.

Tess's face was full of surprise and apprehension as d'Urberville asked her to mount his gig and drive with him to The Slopes. She wanted to ride in the cart. But, when she looked down the hill at her family, she thought about Prince and how she was responsible for his death. Then she climbed onto the gig with Alec d'Urberville.

As they drove along, Alec paid many compliments to Tess. Joan had insisted that Tess dress in her best clothes. Sitting on the gig in her white muslin dress with a pink ribbon in her hair, Tess wished she had worn her ordinary working clothes. She had a full figure that made her look more of a woman and less of a child than she really was, and the white muslin dress emphasised this. Tess looked out at the green valley of her birth and the grey unfamiliar countryside beyond.

'Will you go slow, sir, when we go downhill?' asked Tess.

'No, Tess,' said d'Urberville, holding his cigar between his strong white teeth and smiling at her. 'I enjoy going down the hills at full gallop!'

As they descended the hill, the gig went faster and faster. The wind blew through Tess's white muslin and chilled her skin. She did not want him to see that she was frightened, but she was afraid of falling off the gig, so she held his arm.

'Don't hold my arm,' said he. 'Hold on around my waist.'

She held his waist, and so they reached the bottom.

'Safe, thank God, in spite of your fooling!' cried Tess.

'Don't be angry, Tess, and don't let go of me now that you are out of danger.'

Tess blushed. She had held onto his waist without thinking.

'Here's another hill! Hang on!'

As the gig sped down the hill, Alec turned to Tess and said,

'Now put your arms around my waist as you did before!'

'Never!' cried Tess independently.

'If you let me kiss you, I'll slow down.'

Tess moved as far away from him as she could. 'Will nothing else make you slow down?' she cried.

'Nothing, dear Tess.'

'Oh! All right!'

He slowed the gig down and leaned over to kiss her, but Tess turned her face away.

'You little witch!' cried Alec. 'I'll drive so fast that we will both be killed, if you don't keep your promise.'

'All right!' said Tess, 'but you should be kind to me, since you are my cousin.'

'Nonsense! Come here!'

'I don't want anyone to kiss me, sir!' cried Tess. A big tear rolled down her cheek, and her lips trembled. 'I wish I had stayed at home!'

When d'Urberville kissed her, she blushed with shame. At that moment, Tess's hat blew off in the wind. 'Oh, sir! Let me get my hat!' she said. He stopped the gig. Tess jumped down, ran back along the road, and picked up her hat.

'Come on! Get back on the gig,' said d'Urberville.

'No, sir,' Tess replied. 'I shall walk.'

'You let your hat blow off deliberately!'

Tess did not deny it. D'Urberville began to swear at her. He drove the gig towards her, forcing her to climb into the hedge.

'You should be ashamed of yourself for using such wicked words!' cried Tess. 'I don't like you at all! I hate you! I'll go back to my mother!'

Alec's anger disappeared at the sight of Tess's. He laughed heartily. 'Well, I like you even more now! Come here, and let there be peace. I won't do it any more against your will, I promise!'

'I won't get back on the gig, sir!' said Tess. She walked along, with the gig moving slowly beside her. In this way they came to The Slopes.

Tess's life at The Slopes was quite pleasant. Her duties were not difficult, and the other workers were friendly. On the first day, Tess was surprised to learn that Mrs d'Urberville was blind. Even so, the old lady was very interested in her chickens and treated them more like pets than farm animals. Every morning Tess brought the chickens to Mrs d'Urberville. The old lady took the chickens in her arms one by one. She recognised each one and called it by its name. Although she was kind and polite to Tess, clearly she had no idea that they were cousins.

Tess often met Alec in the house or the garden. Sometimes it seemed that he was following her, watching her secretly from behind walls and curtains. She was reserved towards him, but he treated her as if they were old friends. He often called her 'cousin', though sometimes his tone was ironic.

On Saturday nights, the villagers went to a nearby market town called Chaseborough to dance, drink beer, and enjoy themselves. At first, Tess refused to go with them, but the others asked her again, and finally she agreed. She enjoyed herself the first time, so she began to go regularly.

One Saturday in September, Tess worked late at the chicken farm, then walked to Chaseborough alone, because her friends had all gone earlier in the evening. By the time she got there, the sun had already set. At first she could not find her friends, then someone told her that they had gone dancing in the barn of a local farmer. As Tess walked along the road to the barn, she saw Alec standing on the corner.

'Why are you out so late, my beauty?' he said.

She told him she was looking for her friends, so that she could walk home with them.

'I'll see you again,' he called to her as she walked on.

The barn was full of yellow light. Tess's friends were dancing with their arms around each other, like satyrs and nymphs. A young man asked her to dance, but she refused. The dancing seemed so mad and passionate, it made Tess uncomfortable.

'Are any of you walking home soon?' she asked anxiously. She was afraid to walk home alone.

'Oh yes,' replied a man. 'This will be the last dance.'

But when that dance was over, the dancers asked the musicians to play once more. Tess waited and waited.

Suddenly, one of the couples in the dance fell down, and other couples fell on top of them. Tess heard a loud laugh behind her. She looked around and saw the red end of a burning cigar in the shadows. Alec was standing there alone.

'Hello, my beauty. What are you doing here?'

Tess explained that she was waiting for her friends to walk home.

'I'm on horseback this evening, but I could rent a gig from the hotel and drive you home,' he said.

'No, thank you,' she said.

When the dance was finally over, Tess and the others walked back towards Trantridge in the moonlight. Many of the men and some of the women were drunk. Two of the women walked unsteadily: a dark beauty named Car Darch, who was known as the Queen of Spades, and her sister, who was known as the Queen of Diamonds. Until recently, the Queen of Spades had been Alec d'Urberville's favourite.

Car Darch fell in the mud on the road. The others laughed at her, and Tess joined in the laughter. Suddenly Car Darch stood up and said to Tess, 'How dare you laugh at me!'

'Everyone was laughing,' Tess replied.

'You think you are better than the rest of us, just because he likes you best now!'

The Queen of Spades closed her hands and held them up towards Tess, ready to fight.

'I shall not fight you,' said Tess, 'I did not know that you were whores! I wish I had not waited to walk home with you!'

This general comment made the others angry too. The Queen of Diamonds, who had also been one of Alec's favourites in the past, united with her sister against the common enemy. Several other women also insulted Tess. Their husbands and lovers tried to make peace by defending her, but this only made the situation worse.

Tess was no longer afraid to walk home alone, she just wanted to get away from these people. Suddenly Alec appeared on horseback out of the shadows. He rode up to Tess, who was standing a little apart from the others.

'What the devil are you people doing?' he cried. 'Jump up on my horse,' he whispered to Tess, 'and we'll be far away from them in a moment.'

She wanted to refuse his help, as she had refused it before. But now she was afraid of these angry drunken companions. She wanted to mount the horse and ride away, triumphing over her enemies. She gave in to the impulse and got on the horse.

As Alec and Tess rode away, Car Darch and her sister began to laugh.

'What are you laughing at?' asked a young man.

Car's mother, who was also laughing, said, 'Out of the frying-pan into the fire!'

Alec and Tess rode along in silence. Tess was glad of her triumph, but she was nervous about her present situation. She held on to Alec's waist as he rode, because she was afraid of falling off. She asked him to ride slowly, and he did so.

'Are you glad to have escaped from them, dear Tess?' asked Alec.

'Yes. I should be grateful to you.'

'And are you?'

She did not reply.

'Tess, why do you not like me to kiss you?'

'Because I don't love you.'

'Are you sure?'

'I am angry with you sometimes!'

'Ah, I thought so,' said Alec sadly, but he was not really saddened by what she had said. He knew that any other feeling she had for him was better than indifference.

They fell silent, and the horse walked on. There was a faint luminous fog around them. They had passed the road to Trantridge a long time ago, but Tess had not noticed. She was tired. This morning, as usual, she had risen at five and worked all day. It was now nearly one o'clock. Fatigue overcame her, and her head sank gently against his back.

D'Urberville stopped the horse, turned around, and put his arm around her waist, but the movement woke Tess, and she pushed him away.

'Good God! You nearly pushed me off the horse!' cried Alec.

'I'm sorry, sir,' said Tess humbly.

'For nearly three months you have treated me this way, Tess, and I won't tolerate it! You know that I love you and think you are the prettiest girl in the world, and yet you treat me badly. Will you not let me act as your lover?'

'I don't know - I wish - how can I say yes or no when...'

Then Tess noticed that the road was unfamiliar. 'Where are we?' she asked.

'We are in The Chase - the oldest forest in England. It's a lovely night, and I thought we could ride for a little longer.'

'How could you be so treacherous! Let me down. I want to walk home.'

'You cannot walk home, darling. We are miles from Trantridge.'

'Never mind. Let me down, sir!'

'All right,' said Alec. 'But I don't know where we are. Promise to wait by the horse while I walk through the woods in search of a road or a house. When I know where we are, I will give you directions and let you walk home alone, or you may ride, if you wish.'

Tess agreed to this plan.

Alec tied the horse to a tree and made a pile of dried leaves on the ground nearby. 'Sit there,' he said. 'I'll be back soon. By the way, Tess, somebody gave your father a new horse today.'

'How very kind of you!' she cried, but she felt embarrassed having to thank him at that moment. 'I almost wish that you had not.'

'Why, dear?'

'It makes things difficult for me.'

'Tessy - don't you love me a little now?'

'I'm grateful,' she reluctantly admitted. 'But I don't love you.'

The knowledge that his passion for her had caused him to be so kind to her family made Tess feel sad, and she began to cry.

'Don't cry, dear! Sit down here and wait for me. Are you cold?'

Tess was wearing only her thin muslin dress. Alec took off his coat and put it over her shoulders, then he walked off into the fog.

He went up the hill so that he could see the surrounding countryside and discover where they were. From the hilltop he saw a familiar road, so he turned back. The moon had now set, and The Chase was dark. At first he could not find the spot where he had left the horse. But, after walking around in the darkness for some time, he heard the sound of the horse moving.

'Tess?'

There was no answer. It was so dark that he could see nothing but the pale cloud of her dress on the ground at his feet. He stooped and heard her gentle regular breathing. He knelt beside her and bent lower till her breath warmed his face and his cheek rested on hers. She was asleep, and there were tears on her eyelashes.

The ancient trees of The Chase rose high above them in darkness and silence. But where was Tess's guardian angel? This coarse young man was about to claim a fine, sensitive, pure girl for his own. Why does this happen so often? Perhaps in this case Nemesis was involved. No doubt some of Tess's noble ancestors had treated the peasant girls of their time in the same way.

Tess's own people, who believe in Fate, often say, 'It was to be.' That was the pity of it.

CHAPTER THREE

Maiden no More

The basket was heavy, but she carried it without complaining: her heaviest burdens were not material things. It was a Sunday morning in late October, a few weeks after Tess's night ride in The Chase. She climbed the hill and looked down into the valley of her birth. Today it seemed even more beautiful than usual. Since she had last seen it, she had learned that the serpent hisses where the sweet birds sing, and her views of life had been totally changed by the lesson. She was now a different girl from the one who had left her home four months earlier.

Alec drove up behind her in a gig. 'Why did you run away?' he asked. 'I had to drive very fast to catch up with you. If you won't come back to Trantridge with me, at least let me take you to your village in the gig.'

'I won't come back.'

'Let me take you home then.'

She put her basket and bundle in the gig and climbed up beside him. She had no fear of him now, and the reason for that was also the cause of her sorrow.

Alec had quite forgotten his struggle to kiss her in June, when they had driven together along the same road in the opposite direction. She had not forgotten, and now she sat with her head down, replying to his remarks in monosyllables.

When the village of Marlott came in sight, Tess began to cry.

'Why are you crying?' he coldly asked.

'I was born there.'

'Well - we were all born somewhere.'

'I wish I had never been born!'

'If you didn't want to come to Trantridge, why did you come? I know you didn't come because you loved me!'

'No, I did not go there because I loved you - I never sincerely loved you. That is why I hate myself for my weakness! I didn't understand your meaning until it was too late.'

'That's what every woman says.'

'How dare you use such words!' she cried, turning to him with a flash of anger. 'Don't you know that what every woman says some women may feel?'

'All right, I admit that I did wrong. But I'm willing to pay for it. You don't need to work ever again. You can buy yourself beautiful clothes.'

'I don't want your money!'

'Well, if you need anything in the future, write to me, and I'll send it to you.'

He stopped the gig and helped her down. They were at the edge of the village now, and she wanted to walk the rest of the way alone. 'Let me kiss you goodbye, Tess,' he said.

'If you wish.' She stood there passively while he kissed first one cheek and then the other.

'You never let me kiss your mouth, though, and you never kiss me back. I'm afraid you'll never love me.'

'No. I'll never love you. Perhaps I should lie about that now. But I have a little honour left, and so I won't tell that lie.'

'Then goodbye, dear cousin,' he said. He leapt onto the gig and was gone.

As Tess walked along the country lane to Marlott, she passed a man who was writing texts from the Bible in bold red paint on a wall. He had already completed one that read, Thy damnation slumbereth not. Now he was writing another: Thou shalt not commit....

Against the soft blues and greys of the landscape, the scarlet letters seemed grotesque, A and their message seemed frightening and horrible.

Then she saw the smoke rising from the chimney of her old home, and her heart ached.

'My dear!' cried her mother, when Tess appeared at the kitchen door. 'Have you come home to be married to your cousin?'

'No,' said Tess quietly. 'He is not my cousin, and he will not marry me.'

'For a holiday, then?'

'Yes.'

Her mother looked at her closely. 'What has happened?' she asked. Tess rested her head against her mother's shoulder and told her everything.

'And yet you didn't get him to marry you!'

'Any woman except me,' said Tess.

'Why didn't you think of your family, instead of thinking only of yourself? Your father is not well, and you see how hard I work. He gave us the horse and many other presents. If he is not your cousin, he must have done it because he loves you. And yet you didn't get him to marry you! You should have been more careful, if you did not want to be his wife.'

'O mother!' cried poor Tess. 'How could I have known? Why didn't you tell me that men were dangerous? Why didn't you warn me?'

Joan said, 'I did not want you to be afraid and lose your chance. Ah, well! We must make the best of it. It is nature, after all. It pleases God!'

Rumours of her wealthy cousin's love for her made other girls in the village admire and envy Tess. As time went by, however, she began to hate the way they looked at her and talked about her in whispers. She left the house less and less frequently. If she wanted to take a walk, she went at dusk, when most people were at home.

During those walks, Tess often saw the birds and the rabbits in the trees and hedges. She felt different from them. She felt that she was Guilt walking through the places of Innocence; but she was wrong to think that. She had been made to break an accepted social law, but she had broken no law of nature.

CHAPTER FOUR

Sorrow

It was a warm morning in August. As the sun rose, the morning mists evaporated. On such a morning it was easy to understand the ancient sun worshippers. There has never been a saner religion! The sun was a golden-haired god, vigorous and young, looking down on the earth with loving interest. His light broke through the cottage windows and awoke those still sleeping. The brightest thing the sun illuminated that morning was the great reaping-machine that stood in the corn field. Soon a group of field workers came down the lane and entered the field. A strange sound came out of the machine, and it began to move slowly. The mechanical reaper passed clown the hill and out of sight. In a minute it came up on the other side of the field. As the machine went round, it cut the corn. Each time it completed a circuit, the area of standing corn left in the middle of the field was smaller. Rabbits, snakes, rats, and mice ran towards the centre of the field.

The reaping-machine left behind it piles of corn, and the field workers followed it, tying the corn into sheaves. The women were more interesting to watch than the men. A field man is a personality in the field; a field woman is a part of the field. Somehow she loses her own boundaries; she absorbs the essence of the landscape and becomes part of it.

The field women wore hats to protect them from the sun and gloves to prevent their hands from being scratched by the stubble. One was wearing a pale pink jacket, another wore a beige dress, and a third had a bright red skirt. The girl in the pale pink jacket was the most interesting. She had the finest figure of all the women there, and her manner was the most reserved. The other women often looked around them, but Tess never raised her eyes from her work.

She tied the sheaves of corn with clock-like monotony.

At eleven o'clock the field workers paused for lunch. Tess's sisters and brothers brought her lunch and the baby. Tess took the baby from her sister, unfastened the front of her dress, and began suckling the child.

When the baby had finished feeding, Tess held it in her arms and looked off into the distance with a sad indifference that was almost dislike. Then suddenly she started kissing the baby with passionate intensity.

'She loves that child,' said the woman in the red skirt, 'even though she says she wishes that both she and the baby had died.'

'Oh,' said the woman in the beige dress. 'She'll get used to it! You get used to anything in time!'

'Some people say they heard a woman crying in The Chase one night last year!'

'What a shame!'

When lunchtime was over, Tess gave the baby to her sister, put on her gloves, and went back to work. All afternoon and evening she continued to bind the sheaves of corn. Then, as the moon rose over the fields, she went back to the village with the other workers. The field women sang songs on the way. One of them invented a new verse about a maid who went into the forest and came back in a changed state. As she sang it, the others smiled at Tess. Touched by the women's friendliness, Tess began to feel a little happier.

When she got home that evening, the baby was ill. This was not surprising: he had been small and weak from birth. Tess was frightened because he had not been baptised.

The family went to sleep, but Tess lay anxiously awake. In the middle of the night, the baby got worse. The clock struck one, that hour when imagination is stronger than reason and malignant possibilities become realities. She imagined the Devil sticking his trident into her baby. The image frightened her so much that she cried out loud: 'Oh merciful God, have pity on my poor baby! Be angry with me, but pity the poor child!'

Then suddenly she had an idea: she lit a candle then went to the other beds in the room and woke her brothers and sisters. She poured some water into the washbasin. She made her brothers and sisters kneel with their hands together in prayer. The children, still half asleep, were full of awe as they watched their sister take her baby from its bed. Tess then stood erect with the baby on her arm. Liza-Lu, the eldest after Tess, held the Prayer Book open. Thus Tess baptised her own child.

Her figure looked tall and imposing as she stood in her long white nightgown. In the gentle candlelight, her eyes flashed with enthusiasm. Her motherhood - which had been her shame - now seemed transfigured into something of immaculate beauty, touched with a dignity that was almost regal. The children looked up at her in awe.

Tess had decided to name the child Sorrow. Now, as she proceeded with the baptismal service, she pronounced it: 'SORROW, baptise you in the name of the Father, and of the Son, and of the Holy Spirit.'

She dropped some water on his head.

'Say "Amen", children.'

'Amen,' said the children obediently.

As she read out the baptismal service, Tess's voice became stronger and more passionate, and her face shone with faith.

In the blue of the morning, poor Sorrow died.

CHAPTER FIVE

The Dairy

Tess stayed with her family all through the winter months. Her experiences had changed her from a simple girl to a complex woman. Her soul was that of a woman who had not been demoralised by her sorrows.

The spring came, with a feeling of germination in the air. It moved Tess with a desire for life. She knew that she could never be comfortable in Marlott again. But if she went somewhere else, where no one knew her history? Tess longed to go. She heard that a dairy farm many miles to the south needed a milkmaid, and she decided to go there. A spirit was rising in her as automatically as the sap in the trees: it was the spirit of youth, and with it came hope.

On a beautiful morning in May, she took a hired cart to the town of Stourcastle. There she took another cart to Talbothay's Dairy. The cart passed by Kingsbere Church, where the d'Urbervilles were buried. Tess no longer admired her ancestors. They were responsible, she felt, for all her troubles. 'I will tell no one in the new place that I am a d'Urberville,' she thought. Yet one of the reasons this particular place attracted her was that it was near the ancestral lands of her family.

She looked with interest as the cart entered the Valley of the Great Dairies, a verdant plain watered by the River Froom. 'This will be my new home!' she thought. The green fields were full of brown and white cattle, grazing peacefully in the evening light. The waters of the River Froom were clear and rapid. Tess felt happy and hopeful. The fresh air and the excitement of a new place made her cheeks pink and her eyes bright.

She reached the dairy at milking-time. The dairy workers in the milk-house watched with interest as Tess approached. The owner of the dairy - Mr Crick - introduced himself to Tess. 'Do you want something to eat before you start milking?' he asked.

'No, thank you,' Tess replied. Mr Crick gave her a stool. She placed it beside a cow, sat down, rested her cheek against the cow's side, and began milking. Soon the only sound in the milk-house was that of warm milk squirting into buckets.

After a little while, the dairy workers began to talk.

'The cows are not giving as much milk as usual,' said one.

'That's because we have someone new in the dairy,' replied another. 'It always happens.'

'We should sing a song to calm their nerves,' said a third.

'You could play your harp to them, sir,' said Mr Crick.

'Why?' asked a voice that seemed to come from the brown cow opposite Tess.

Then a dairy-worker told a story about a man being chased by a bull. The man had his fiddle with him, and he played music to calm the bull. The bull stood still. Then the man played a Christmas song, and the bull got down on his knees.

'What a strange story!' said the voice from behind the brown cow. 'It is like a story from medieval times, when faith was a living thing!'

Tess wondered who the speaker was. Why did the others call him 'sir'? Finally he stood up. 'I think I have finished this one,' he said. 'Though she made my fingers ache.'

Tess could now see him. He wore the usual clothes of a dairyman, but there was something educated, reserved, sad, and different about him. Suddenly she realised that she had seen him before.

He was the young gentleman who had not asked her to dance in the field at Marlott that day, so long ago, before all her troubles began.

That night Tess went to bed in a large room over the milk-house, which she shared with three other milkmaids. Retty, who had the bed next to Tess, kept talking about Talbothay's and all the people there: 'That young gentleman - the one who is learning to milk and plays the harp - is Mr Angel Clare. He's a parson's son. His father is the Reverend Clare at Emminster. His brothers will become parsons like their father, but Mr Angel wants to be a farmer.'

Tess was too tired to ask her neighbour questions. Gradually she fell asleep to the sound of her voice and the smell of the cheeses stored in the cheese-room next door.

Angel was the youngest and brightest of the Reverend Clare's three sons. But he had disappointed his father. The Reverend Clare had wished all three of his sons to become parsons like himself, but Angel had refused.

'Father, I do not want to join the clergy,' he had said one day. 'I love the Church as one loves a parent, but I have doubts about several of her doctrines.'

'If you refuse to join the clergy, you can't go to Cambridge. The purpose of a university education is to help one work for the glory of God.'

'It can help one work for the glory of man, too, father,' said Angel. 'But I will do without Cambridge.'

He went to London and became involved with a woman much older than himself who nearly trapped him into marriage. Finally, disgusted with the city, he returned to the purity of the countryside and decided to learn all aspects of farming. So we find Angel Clare, at the age of twenty-six, learning how to milk cows in Talbothay's Dairy, renting a large attic room from Mr Crick, and eating his meals with the dairy workers.

At first he had chosen farming as a way of earning his living without giving up his intellectual freedom. Then gradually he came to love farm life. He liked the farm workers and took an interest in their characters and beliefs. He began to pay attention to the seasons and the changes of weather, morning and evening, night and noon, trees, mists, silences, and the voices of inanimate things.

One morning, a few days after Tess's arrival at Talbothay's, Angel was sitting reading a book over his breakfast when he heard an unfamiliar voice. 'What a musical voice that is,' he thought. 'It must be the new milkmaid.'

'I don't know about ghosts, but I do know that our souls can leave our bodies when we are alive.'

'Really?' said Mr Crick, turning to Tess in surprise.

'If you lie on the grass at night and look straight up at the stars, you feel as if you are hundreds of miles away from your body.' Tess noticed that everyone, including Mr Clare, was listening to her. She blushed.

Clare continued to observe her. 'What a fresh and virginal daughter of Nature!' he said to himself. He thought perhaps he had seen her somewhere before, but he could not remember where. But he began to think of Tess more than any of the other pretty milkmaids.

CHAPTER SIX

Love Grows

One evening in June, as Tess was walking in the garden, she heard Angel playing his harp. Although he was not a very good player, Tess was fascinated. She followed the music, stepping softly through the wet grasses and weeds, sending mists of pollen up into the air.

She stopped quite near to him, but he did not see her. The sounds of his harp passed through her like warm winds. Her body moved gently to the music, and her eyes filled with tears.

The tune ended, and Tess realised with alarm that he was walking towards her. She turned to go, but he called out to her, 'Why do you hurry away, Tess? Are you afraid?'

'Oh no, sir, not of outdoor things.'

'But you are afraid of indoor things?'

'Well - yes, sir.'

'What things?'

'I can't say.'

'Life in general?'

'Yes, sir.'

'Ah - I am often afraid of that too. But why should a young girl like you feel that way?'

She was silent.

'Come, Tess, tell me. I promise I will tell no one else.'

'I seem to see a long line of tomorrows getting smaller and smaller in the distance. They all seem very cruel. They all seem to say, "I'm coming! Beware of me!"'

He was surprised that she had such sad imaginings. She seemed to be expressing, in her own simple way, the feelings of the age - the pain of modernism. What we call advanced ideas, he thought, are really just the latest definition of sensations that men and women have been feeling for centuries. Still, it was strange that such ideas had come to her while she was still so young. It was more than strange: it was impressive, interesting, and pathetic.

Tess thought it strange that a well-educated young gentleman could be afraid of life in general. Why did such an admirable poetic man not feel it a blessing to be alive? Certainly he was now working outside his social class, but he did so of his own free will. Still, she wondered why such a book-loving, musical, thoughtful young man should decide to be a farmer and not a parson, like his father and brothers.

Every day, every hour, he learned one more little thing about her and she about him. At first she thought of him as an intellect rather than as a man. She compared her own modest world view to his and felt discouraged. One day, when he was talking about the ancient Greeks, he noticed that she looked sad.

'What's the matter, Tess?' he asked.

'I was just thinking about myself. My life has been wasted. When I see how much you have read and seen and thought, I feel what a nothing I am!'

'Don't worry about that. I will help you learn anything you want to learn. I could teach you history, for example,' said Angel with enthusiasm.

'No.'

'Why not?'

'I don't want to learn that I am just one of many. I don't want to read books that tell me that my thoughts and actions are just like those of thousands of other people before me.'

'Don't you want to learn anything?'

'I want to know why the sun shines on the just and the unjust alike,' she answered in a trembling voice. 'But they don't teach that in books.'

'Don't be so bitter, Tess,' said Angel, although he had often felt the same way in the past. He looked at the side of her face and noticed the curl of her eyelashes and the softness of her cheek. Reluctantly he went away.

When he was gone, Tess felt angry with herself. How stupid he must think her! She wanted him to like her. She thought about her noble ancestors. The next day, Tess asked Mr Crick if Mr Clare had respect for old noble families.

'Oh no!' replied Mr Crick emphatically. 'Mr Clare is a rebel! He hates old families. He says that they used up all their strength in the past and have nothing left now. He thinks that is why so many old families around here have lost their wealth and become common people. One of our dairymaids - Retty Priddle - is descended from the Paridelles, an old family that once owned lots of land around here. When Mr Clare found this out, he was very severe with the poor girl. "You'll never be a good milkmaid," he said, "because your family wasted all its strength fighting wars in the Middle Ages." And, some time ago, a boy came to ask for a job. He said his name was Matt. We asked him what his surname was, and he said he didn't have one. We asked him why, and he replied, "Well, I suppose my family has not been established long enough." When Mr Clare heard that, he jumped up and shook the boy's hand, saying, "You're exactly the kind of boy we want!"'

Tess was glad she had not told Angel about her family. Now she knew he did not respect old families. Besides, another dairymaid was as good as she in that respect. The story about the boy made Tess suspect that Angel was interested in her only because he thought that she too was from a new family.

The summer matured, producing a new generation of flowers, nightingales, and other ephemeral creatures. The sunlight made flowers open and sap rise in the trees. The warmth of the sun filled the air with perfumes. Life at Talbothay's Dairy went on comfortably. Tess and Clare watched each other. They were balanced on the edge of passion. They were moving irresistibly towards each other, like two rivers in one valley.

Tess had never been so happy. One reason was that the life she lived now was completely appropriate for her. The other reason was that she, like Angel, was not yet aware of being in love. She was not yet at the stage when one asks oneself disturbing questions: Where will this new feeling carry me? What effect will it have on my future? What relation does it have to my past?

They met every day at dawn. It was Tess's job to wake the other dairy workers, and every morning she climbed the ladder to Angel's attic room and called him in a loud whisper. He rose immediately, got dressed, and went downstairs. All the other dairy workers slept for another fifteen minutes before rising. So usually Tess and Angel spent the first fifteen minutes of the day together, alone, out in the humid air and the rosy light of dawn. Sometimes it seemed to them that they were Adam and Eve, alone on the earth.

The soft light of those mornings often reminded him of the Resurrection hour, though he never imagined that the Magdalen was by his side. The early-morning light gave her face a radiant quality, so that she looked ghostly, like a soul walking free of its body. It was then she impressed him most deeply. She was no longer a milkmaid: she seemed to him the essence of womanhood. He called her Artemis and Demeter. She did not like this, because she did not understand the references.

'Call me Tess,' she said, and he did.

One evening, Tess went to bed early. She fell asleep, but a little later she was woken by the sounds of the other three milkmaids who shared her room. She opened her eyes and saw them looking out of the window together, watching someone in the garden below.

'Don't push! You can see as well as I can,' said Retty, the youngest of the three.

'It's useless for you or me to be in love with him,' said Marian, the eldest. 'He loves someone else.'

'Izz loves him too,' said Retty. 'I saw her kissing his shadow on the milk-house wall.'

Izz blushed. 'Well, I do love him, but so do you, and so does Marian.'

Marian's round face was always very pink; now it became even pinker. 'But he likes Tess best,' she said. 'I've seen him watching her.'

'He won't marry any of us,' said Izz. 'He is a gentleman, and we are just milkmaids.'

Tess lay in her bed and thought about Angel. One day she had heard Mr Crick joking with him. Mr Crick had said, 'You will marry a fine lady, sir!' But Angel had replied, 'No, I won't. Perhaps I will marry a farm-woman - someone who can help me on the farm.' But Tess knew that she - with her terrible secret - could never marry anyone now.

From that day on, Tess tried to avoid Angel's company. When she was with him, she drew his attention to the other milkmaids.

'They blush when you look at them,' she said. 'Why don't you marry one of them?' She felt that this was the right thing to do. What right had she - who could not marry anyone - to enjoy the sunshine of his smiles? Now that she knew the other milkmaids loved him, she felt it was her duty to give them a chance of winning his love. Nevertheless, it broke her heart to do so.

The hot weather of July came, then the rains began. It rained heavily and frequently. The fields were wet, and the streams were full.

One Sunday morning, after the milking was done, Tess and the other three milkmaids decided to go to Mellstock Church. It had rained heavily the night before, but now the sun was shining. Walking along the lane to Mellstock, the girls came to a place where the rain had flooded the road. On weekdays, they simply walked through the water, but today they were wearing their best shoes.

Suddenly they saw Angel Clare walking towards them through the water.

'Are you trying to get to the church?' he asked. 'If you want, I will carry you over.'

The four girls blushed.

'You can't carry me, sir. I'm too heavy,' said Marian.

'Nonsense!' said Angel. 'Put your arms around my shoulders. That's right! Now off we go!'

He walked back across the flood with Marian in his arms, then returned to the other three. One by one, he carried the blushing milkmaids across the water. He left Tess till last.

'You must be so tired, Mr Clare. Perhaps I can walk around the flood.'

'No, Tess,' he replied. 'I carried the others just so that I could have the pleasure of carrying you.'

CHAPTER SEVEN

The Consequence

August was hot. At midday the landscape seemed paralysed by the heat. Angel found the heat oppressive, but he was even more troubled by his growing passion for the soft and silent Tess.

Now they milked the cows in the fields, for coolness and convenience. One afternoon, at milking-time, Angel found Tess in a secluded corner of the field, milking one of the cows. He placed his stool beside a nearby cow and sat down. But he did not start milking. Instead he watched Tess. She was leaning her cheek against the flank of the cow. Her face in profile was like a delicate cameo against the brown background of the cow. Her eyes gazed dreamily off to the horizon. The picture was still, except for Tess's hands, which moved gently and rhythmically, like the beating of a heart.

How lovable her face was to him. It was full of vitality and warmth. He loved her eloquent eyes, her fair skin, her arched brows, and the beautiful shape of her chin and throat. Above all he loved her mouth. It reminded him of that image in Elizabethan poetry of the beloved's lips and teeth like roses filled with snow. He was tempted to call Tess's mouth perfect, but no, it was not perfect. And that touch of imperfection gave it sweetness and humanity.

Overcome with emotion, Angel leapt up and knelt beside her. He put his arms around her. She was surprised, but, when she saw it was he, she yielded to his embrace with a cry of pleasure.

'Forgive me, Tess dear!' he whispered. 'I should have asked. I love you!'

Tess's eyes filled with tears.

Just then they heard Mr Crick approaching. They went back to their milking as if nothing had happened. But something had happened. The universe had changed for Angel and Tess.

Angel's embrace had been impulsive. Afterwards he was amazed and frightened by what he had done. But now it was clear to him that she loved him. Why should he not marry her?

The next day he went to Emminster to discuss it with his family. His parents were not enthusiastic about him marrying a milkmaid. They wanted him to marry Mercy Chant, the daughter of a neighbouring clergyman.

'Ah, well!' said the Reverend Clare finally. 'I suppose a farmwoman will be a better wife for you than a fine lady. And I am glad to hear you say that she is a good Christian.'

Angel got back to Talbothay's at three o'clock. The dairy workers were taking their afternoon nap. The first to wake up was Tess. She descended the stairs, yawning, and Angel saw the red interior of her mouth, like a snake's. When she saw him she was startled: 'O Mr Clare! You frightened me !'

Angel put his arms around her. 'Darling Tessy!' he whispered. 'Don't call me Mister any more. I have hurried back from Emminster to ask you something very important. Will you be my wife?'

Tess went pale. 'No - I cannot,' she murmured.

'Don't you love me?'

'O yes!'

'Then why won't you marry me?'

Tess was forced to invent a reason: 'Your family won't like it. I am just a milkmaid.'

'But that is why I went home, Tessy. I told them about you, and they have agreed to our marriage.'

'But I cannot agree!'

'Was it too sudden, Tessy? Do you need time to think about it?'

'Yes,' she said, relieved.

So Angel did not ask again for a few days. A terrible struggle was going on in Tess's heart. She knew that, as an honourable woman, she must refuse him. But she wanted so much to accept him! The other milkmaids noticed her distress I and guessed that something important had happened.

On Sunday he asked her again, and again she refused. 'One day she will accept me,' thought Angel with confidence. Therefore he was patient and loving.

Days and weeks went by. September came and went. Occasionally Angel asked his question again. She tried, on one or two occasions, to tell him her terrible secret, but she failed. She was afraid of losing his love.

One day Angel volunteered to drive the milk to the station. He asked Tess to accompany him, and she accepted.

"Tess,' he said, as they drove along. 'You must tell me why you refuse to marry me.'

'It is for your own good,' Tess replied. 'It is to do with my past.'

'Tell me.'

'Well, a few years ago,' Tess began, 'my family was in trouble. We were very poor, and my father drank a little -'

'That's not unusual,' said Angel.

'But there was something unusual. Our family is descended from the d'Urbervilles - '

'Really? Is that all? Is that the reason you refuse me?' Angel laughed and stopped the cart.

Poor Tess did not have the strength to tell the rest of her story. 'Yes,' she said. 'Mr Crick told me that you hated old families.'

'Well, it's true that I hate the privileges of aristocracy, but that makes no difference to us. Now, will you marry me?'

'Yes!' cried Tess, and she burst into tears.

Angel was surprised. There was nothing hysterical in Tess's nature. 'Why are you crying, dearest?' he asked.

'Oh! I wish I had never been born!' said the poor girl.

'Tess! Don't you love me? Why are you so sad?'

'Of course I love you,' Tess replied. She put her arms around his neck and, for the first time, Angel tasted the kisses of an impassioned woman who loved him with all her heart and soul.

The next day Tess wrote a letter to her mother, asking her advice. Joan wrote back immediately, saying that Tess should never tell Angel about her past troubles. Tess realised that her mother's views of life were superficial. But she thought her advice was sound.

'Tess has agreed to marry me!' said Angel to the people at Talbothay's the next day. 'We will buy our own farm in the English Midlands and be married in December.'

Tess watched the other milkmaids nervously. 'Now they will hate me!' she thought. But that night, in their bedroom, Retty, Izz, and Marian all crowded round her. They embraced and kissed her, looking at her in wonder, amazed that a simple milkmaid was going to be his wife. Tess was moved by their goodness. That night she wept silently. 'I will tell Angel my secret after all!' she thought. 'He is so good, and they are so good. I must be good too!'

Tess adored Angel. Sometimes he caught her gazing at him with eyes full of love. They spent all their free time together now. Throughout the month of October, they went for walks in the afternoons. In the autumn sunshine, they walked by the river and planned their future.

In November, however, Angel changed his plans. During a visit to the Wellbridge flourmill, he decided to spend some time there after leaving Talbothay's. There he could learn all about the milling of flour, but that was not the reason he decided to go. He made the decision when he discovered that the farmhouse there was an old mansion that once belonged to the d'Urbervilles. Angel thought it was the perfect place for their honeymoon.

One day they went into the village to do some Christmas shopping. Tess waited outside the inn, while Angel went to get the horse and gig. Two men came out of the inn while Tess was waiting.

'What a pretty maid!' said one.

'Yes,' said the other, looking at her closely. She thought he was a Trantridge man. 'She is pretty. But, unless I am mistaken...'

Tess did not hear the rest of what he said, but Angel did. He was coming back from the stables and passed the man as he spoke. The insult infuriated Angel. He struck the man on the chin.

'I made a mistake,' said the man. 'I thought she was another woman.'

As the wedding day approached, Tess thought about her confession. 'O, when and how can I tell him?' she asked herself again and again. One night she heard a noise in Angel's room. She went to see what was the matter.

'I'm sorry I woke you, Tess,' said Angel. 'I dreamt I was fighting with that man again.' The noise you heard was me hitting the bed. I sometimes do strange things like that in my sleep.' Now Tess felt that she must confess everything to Angel. She decided to write him a letter.

On the evening before the wedding, Tess wrote the letter, explaining all her past sorrows. She crept up the attic stairs and put the letter under Angel's door.

The next morning, he greeted her with his usual warmth and affection. 'He can't have read my letter,' thought Tess, and she ran up the attic stairs to his room. The letter was still there. Tess had pushed it under the door, but it had gone under the carpet. Angel had not seen it. He still knew nothing of her past.

That day was full of preparations for the wedding. She tried to talk to him when they met on the stairs, knowing it was her last chance to confess before their marriage. 'Don't worry, my dear,' Angel said 'We will tell each other all our faults this evening, after the wedding, when we are alone together.'

And so they were married. They left the church in a coach that Angel had rented. As Tess approached it, she said, 'I've seen this coach somewhere before.'

'Perhaps you have heard the legend of the d'Urberville coach,' said Angel, 'and this one reminds you of it.'

'No. I haven't heard. Tell me.'

'Well - a d'Urberville of the sixteenth century committed a terrible crime in the family coach. Ever since, members of the family see the coach whenever - but let's not think of sad things.'

'Do we see the coach when we are going to die or when we have committed a crime?'

'Never mind,' said Angel, silencing her with a kiss.

Back at the dairy, Tess went up to her old bedroom to change her clothes. She knelt down and tried to pray to God, but instead she prayed to Angel: 'O my dear! The woman you love is not my real self but the woman I might have been!'

When the time came to leave Talbothay's, Mr Crick and the dairy workers came out to wave goodbye to them as they drove off. The three milkmaids watched sadly as Tess and Angel got onto the gig. Then a cock crew.

'A cock crowing in the afternoon!' exclaimed Mr Crick.

'That's bad,' said one of the dairymen.

The cock crew again, pointing its beak straight at Clare.

'I don't want to hear it. Drive on,' said Tess to her husband.

He drove away, and everyone called out 'Goodbye! Goodbye!'

Then the cock crew again.

Mr Crick turned towards the bird, crying, 'Stop that noise!'

'It only means that the weather is changing,' said a milkmaid. 'Not what you think: that's impossible!'

'Welcome to your ancestral mansion!' said Angel, when they arrived at the house in Wellbridge. There was no one there except a servant. 'The farmer who lives here has gone to visit friends,' Angel told Tess. 'So, for the first few days, we will have the entire house to ourselves.'

The servant led them upstairs. Tess was startled by two large portraits hanging on the wall. 'What horrible women!' she cried. One of the women had a long pointed face. The expression in her eyes suggested cruel treachery. The other had large teeth and an arrogant expression.

'Who are the women in those portraits?' said Angel.

'Ladies of the d'Urberville family,' the servant replied.

Angel noticed that, despite their unpleasant features and expressions, these women resembled Tess. He regretted that he had chosen this house for their honeymoon.

They washed their hands in the same basin. 'Which are your fingers, and which are mine?' asked Angel playfully.

'They are all yours,' Tess replied.

'How sweet she is!' he thought. 'And now she depends on me entirely for her happiness. I will never neglect her or hurt her!'

The servant prepared their supper and then went home. The sun set, and the wind made strange noises outside the house. It began to rain.

'That cock knew that the weather was changing,' said Angel.

He saw that Tess was still anxious and sad, so he took a package out of his pocket. 'Look, Tess. My father sent a wedding present for you.' He handed her the package. Tess opened it and found a necklace, bracelets, and earrings. She was afraid to touch them at first, but her eyes sparkled.

'Are they mine?' she asked.

'Yes. When my godmother died, she left these jewels for my wife. Put them on.' When Tess was wearing the jewels, Angel stepped back to look at her. 'How beautiful you are!'

Just then there was a knock at the door. Angel went downstairs and let in the man who had brought their luggage from Talbothay's. 'You're late, Jonathan,' said Angel.

'Well, terrible things have been happening at the Dairy since you and your wife left this afternoon. Retty Priddle tried to kill herself. She threw herself in the pond and nearly drowned.'

CHAPTER EIGHT

The Woman Pays

Her narrative ended. She had not tried to excuse herself, and she had not wept. The fire seemed like a demon, laughing at her fate.

Angel stood up and began walking around the room. His face was pale and haggard. 'Why didn't you tell me this before?' he asked. 'Ah! Now I remember. You tried, but I interrupted you.'

'In the name of our love, forgive me!' she whispered with a dry mouth. 'I have forgiven you for the same. Forgive me as you are forgiven, forgive you, Angel.'

'Yes, you do.'

'But you do not forgive me?'

'O Tess, forgiveness does not apply to this case! You were one person, and now you are another.'

He began to laugh. It was as unnatural and horrible as a laugh in hell.

'Oh stop!' cried Tess. 'Forgive me! I thought that you loved me - me, my very self! I love you, and my love will never change. How can you stop loving me?'

'The woman I have been loving is not you.'

Tess burst into a flood of self-pitying tears. He waited patiently and apathetically until she stopped crying.

'I cannot stay here. I will go for a walk.' Saying this, Angel left the room.

Tess followed him, a few steps behind, with dumb and vacant fidelity. After a while she spoke. 'Angel, I am not the deceitful woman you think I am!'

'Not deceitful, my wife, but not the same.'

'I was a child when it happened!'

'I know.'

'Then you forgive me?'

'I do forgive you, but forgiveness is not all.'

'And love me?'

He did not answer.

'Mother says it happens often, and husbands forgive wives.'

'Don't argue, Tess. Different societies have different manners. You sound like an ignorant peasant woman who does not understand social things.'

'I am only a peasant by position, not by nature!'

'That parson should have kept silent about your family. I am sure that your lack of prudence is linked to your descent. I thought you were a fresh child of Nature, but really you are the last descendant of a decadent aristocracy!'

They walked for hours in silence. At one point, Tess said, 'You can divorce me.'

'No I can't. Tess, you know nothing of the law.'

'I don't want to cause you misery for the rest of your life. The river is down there. I will drown myself. I am not afraid.'

'I don't want to add murder to my other errors,' he replied. 'Just go back to the house and go to bed.'

She obeyed. When she lay down on her bed, Tess soon fell asleep. Later Clare returned to the house. He listened at her bedroom door and heard the rhythmic breathing of sleep. 'Thank God!' he thought. But he felt bitter too: having moved the burden of her life onto his shoulders, she was now sleeping soundly. This was partly but not completely true.

He turned away to descend the stairs and went to sleep on the sofa in the sitting room.

For the next three days, they lived together in the house. Yet they were farther apart than they had ever been. Tess made sure the meals were ready on time and tried to keep calm. Clare spent most of the day at the mill. 'Perhaps,' thought Tess,' being together in this house day and night will finally overcome his antipathy.' But Clare did not touch her. He turned away when she offered her lips for a kiss. His love for her had always been rather ideal and ethereal, nothing like the strong honest passion she had for him. Finally, Tess said to him, 'I suppose you will not live with me long, will you, Angel?' Her mouth trembled as she spoke, but she tried to control the trembling.

'We have to stay together for a few days to avoid a scandal,' Clare replied. 'But I cannot live with you long without despising myself and perhaps despising you. How can we live together while that man is still alive? He is your husband in Nature. If we have children, one day they will learn about your past. Sooner or later, someone will tell them. Then they will be disgraced too.'

'I never thought of that,' said Tess. 'You must go away from me, Angel. I will go home to my parents.'

'Do you want to go home?'

'I want to leave you and go home.'

'All right. We will leave here tomorrow morning and go our separate ways.'

That night at midnight, Tess heard a noise on the stairs. She saw the door of her bedroom open. Angel came in and crossed the stream of moonlight from the window. At first Tess felt a flush of joy. She thought he had relented after all. But then she noticed that his eyes were fixed in an unnatural stare. When he reached the middle of the room, he stopped and murmured, in tones of indescribable sadness, 'Dead! Dead! Dead!'

Her love for him was so deep that she could never be afraid of him. He came closer and bent over her. 'Dead! Dead! Dead!' he cried.

He put the sheet around her and lifted her from the bed. Then he carried her across the room, murmuring, 'My poor Tess - so sweet, so good, so true!'

These words of affection brought tears to Tess's eyes. He had been so cold to her in the past three days, and her heart was hungry for love. Angel began to descend the stairs, whispering, 'My wife - dead, dead!'

He stopped and leaned over the banister. 'Maybe he will drop me!' thought Tess. 'Or perhaps he will jump with me in his arms! Then we will die together.' Tess was not afraid.

He kissed her. Then, holding her more tightly, he descended the stairs and walked out into the moonlight. 'Where is he going?' Tess wondered, but still she was not afraid. 'Tomorrow we will part, perhaps for ever'. She found comfort in the fact that he now claimed her as his wife. She was his absolute possession. He could hurt her if he chose.

Ah! Now she knew what he was dreaming of! That Sunday morning when he had carried all four milkmaids over the water.

He walked to the edge of the river. 'Is he going to drown me?' thought Tess. 'Drowning will be better than parting tomorrow.' A plank of wood was placed across the river as a crude bridge. Clare walked over it with Tess in his arms. The waters ran rapidly beneath them. On the other side of the river was a ruined church. Clare carried Tess into it. The empty stone coffin of an abbot stood against the north wall. Clare crossed the church and gently laid Tess in the abbot's coffin. He kissed her again and sighed with relief. Then he lay down on the ground beside the coffin and went to sleep.

Tess sat up in the coffin. It was too cold to leave him where he was. 'Let's walk on, darling,' she whispered, taking him by the arm. He stood up again and followed her. She took him back to the house. In the sitting room she built a fire to warm him. Then she told him to lie down on the sofa. He obeyed, and she covered him with blankets.

The next morning it was clear that Angel remembered nothing of the night before. She thought of telling him what had happened, but then decided not to. After breakfast the carriage arrived to take them as far as Nuttlebury together. Tess saw that carriage as the beginning of the end - at least a temporary end. His tenderness during the night had given her some hope for the future.

Back home in Marlott, Tess put her head on her mother's shoulder and cried, 'You told me not to tell him, but I did, and he went away!'

'Oh you little fool!' said Joan.

Tears ran down Tess's cheeks. The tension of the past four days had been released at last. 'I know!' she cried. 'But I could not deceive him! He was so good, and I loved him so.'

'Well, you deceived him enough to marry him first!'

'Yes. I thought that, if he could not forgive me, he could divorce me. But he told me that I don't understand the law at all. Oh mother, I wanted him so much, but I also wanted to be fair to him!'

'Well, well!' said Joan, with a tear in her eye. 'I don't know why my children are more stupid than other people's. Your poor father has been telling everyone at The Pure Drop that you're married and now we will be rich.'

Meanwhile, Angel went to his family at Emminster. He told his parents nothing of his trouble. He said that he had decided to go to Brazil to start a farm there. 'Tess will stay with her family,' he said, 'and come to Brazil later, when I have a home ready for her.'

He said goodbye to his parents, then returned to the farmhouse at Wellbridge to pay the rent. He spent the night in the room where Tess had slept. In the morning, he prepared to leave for Brazil. 'O Tess!' he whispered to the empty room. 'Why didn't you tell me sooner?'

Just then he heard a knock on the door. It was Izz Huet.

'I came to see you and Mrs Clare,' she said.

'I am here alone,' said Clare. 'I am just leaving. Can I give you a ride anywhere?'

Izz blushed. 'Yes, please,' she said. 'You can take me back to the village. I don't work at Talbothay's anymore. It was so sad there after you left.'

As they drove along, Clare said, 'I am going to Brazil.'

'Does Mrs Clare like the idea?'

'I am going alone. She will join me in a year or two.'

They rode along in silence for a while.

'You look sad, Izz. Why is that?'

'I've been sad for a long time now, sir.'

'And why is that?'

Izz looked at him quickly with pain in her eyes.

'Izz! How weak of you!' he said.

They approached the village, and Clare stopped the gig. 'I am going to Brazil alone,' he said. 'I have separated from my wife for personal reasons. Perhaps

I will never live with her again. I may not be able to love you, Izz, but will you go to Brazil with me?'

'Yes!'

'Do you love me very much, Izz?'

'I do!'

'More than Tess?'

She shook her head. 'No,' she murmured. 'No one could love you more than Tess did!'

Clare was silent. His heart ached. 'Forget our idle talk, Izz,' he said.

Izz burst into tears.

'Be always as good and sincere as you have been today.' He helped her down from the gig.

'Heaven bless you, sir!' she cried.

That night Clare took the ship for Brazil.

It was the October after Clare and Tess had parted. Tess had left Marlott again and had found work as a milkmaid in another village. She preferred this to living on the money that Clare had left her. But then the milking stopped, and she had to look for other work. Weeks passed when she had no work and was forced to spend the money he had left her. Soon it was all gone. Angel's bank sent her another thirty pounds, but Tess sent the money to her family. Her mother had written, saying that they could not pay their debts.

Now Tess had no money. Angel had told her to go to his father if she needed money, but Tess was reluctant to go. And so she moved from farm to farm, taking whatever work she could find.

One day Tess received a letter from Marian. Izz had told her of Tess's trouble, and Marian wrote to tell Tess that the farm where she was working now needed more help. Tess decided to join Marian. As she was walking along a country lane on her way to the new farm, a man came up behind her.

'Hello!' he said. It was the man Angel had hit outside the inn that night in December. 'Aren't you the young woman who was Mr d'Urberville's friend a few years ago?'

Tess did not reply.

'I think you should apologise for that night when your gentleman-friend hit me. What I said was true.'

Tess ran away from him. She ran into the wood and kept running until she felt safe. There, exhausted, she lay down on a pile of dry leaves and fell asleep.

She woke before dawn and lay there, half-asleep. She imagined strange noises around her. She thought of her husband in a hot climate on the other side of the world, while she was here in the cold. 'All is vanity,' she said to herself. But then she thought, 'No. It is worse than that: all is injustice, punishment, and death.'

That day the weather was bad, but Tess continued on her journey. The following evening, she reached the farm where Marian worked. The place was called Flintcomb-Ash, and the countryside there was dry and ugly. There were no trees, and the wind blew harshly. The labour needed on this farm was the hardest kind of field work. As she approached the farm, Tess met Marian on the road. Marian was even fatter and more red-faced than before, and her clothes were old and dirty.

'Tess!' cried Marian. 'How cold and tired you look! But you are a gentleman's wife. It is not fair that you should live like this.'

'Please tell nobody that I am married. I want to work. Do they still need help here?'

'Yes, but it's a miserable place. The work is hard and the weather is bad.'

'You work here, Marian.'

'Yes. I started drinking after you left Talbothay's. It's my only comfort, but, because of my drinking, I can only get the roughest work now.'

The farmer was away, so Marian introduced Tess to the farmer's wife, who was glad to give her a job. Then Tess went into town and found lodgings. That night, in her room, she wrote a letter to her mother, but she did not tell her about the poor conditions in which she was now living. She did not wish to give anyone reason to criticise her husband.

The work at Flintcomb-Ash was very hard indeed. They had to harvest swedes. The cattle had eaten all the leaves above ground, so the field was brown and desolate. The workers had to dig the swedes out of the stony earth. Day after day they worked in the wind and the rain. Then the snow came, and the air was freezing cold.

One day, the farmer returned and came to watch the women working in the field. He stood beside Tess, watching her with interest. When she looked up, she saw that he was the man Angel had hit, the man she had run away from on the road. 'You thought you had escaped me when you ran away that day, but now you are working on my farm! I think you should apologise to me,' he said.

'And I think you should apologise to me,' replied Tess.

From then on, life on the farm was even more difficult for Tess than it had been before.

One evening, Marian and Tess sat together, talking about the old life at Talbothay's. Marian was drinking gin, and, as always when she drank, her thoughts turned to love.

'I did love him so!' said Marian. 'I didn't mind when he married you, but this news about Izz is too bad!'

'What news?'

'O dear! Izz told me not to tell you, but I can't help it. He asked Izz to go to Brazil with him.'

Tess went pale. 'And she refused?'

'I don't know. Anyway, he changed his mind.'

That night, Tess tried to write a letter to Angel, but she could not. How could she write to him when he had asked Izz to go to Brazil with him so soon after their parting? Why had he not written to her? She thought perhaps she ought to go to his parents in Emminster. She could go to his parents' house, ask them for news of him, and express her grief at his silence.

The following Sunday, she dressed in her best clothes and set out for Emminster very early in the morning. As she walked through the crisp morning air, her heart was full of hope. 'I will tell his mother my whole history. Perhaps that lady will pity me and help me to win Angel back.' Gradually the landscape became gentler and greener, the fields smaller. At noon she stood on the hill above Emminster.

All the hope she had felt on the journey now drained away. She walked timidly to the door of Reverend Clare's house and rang the bell. No one answered. Then she realised they must all be at church. 'I will walk up the hill and wait until they have finished their lunch,' thought Tess. As she was walking up the hill, the church doors opened and the congregation emerged.

A young man, walking behind Tess, began speaking to his companion. Tess noticed that his voice was very like Angel's. 'Look!' said he. That's Mercy Chant walking up the hill. Let's join her.'

Tess had heard that name before. Angel's parents had wanted him to marry Mercy Chant. Tess looked up the hill and saw a young woman in plain dark clothes.

'Every time I see Mercy,' continued the young man behind her, 'I think what a great mistake Angel made when he married that milkmaid.'

'It certainly was a mistake,' said his companion. 'But Angel always had strange ideas.'

Tess hurried back along the road to Flintcomb-Ash. She no longer had the courage to speak to Mr and Mrs Clare. The brothers were so cold and unpleasant. And they clearly did not love poor Angel. She grieved for the beloved man whose conventional ideas had caused all her recent sorrow.

CHAPTER NINE

The Convert

Tess walked back from Emminster to Flintcomb-Ash, she saw a crowd of people around a barn. 'What is happening?' she asked a woman there. 'We've all come to listen to the preaching,' the woman replied. 'They say his sermons are very fiery!'

Tess went closer to the barn. She could not see the speaker, but she could hear him. He was calling sinners to repentance, warning them about the fires of hell. Then he began to tell his own history. He said he had been the greatest of sinners. Then one day he met a clergyman - the Reverend Clare of Emminster - who tried to call him to repentance. At first he had ignored Mr Clare's preaching, but finally he was converted and gave up his evil ways.

The voice was more startling to Tess than its message. It was the voice of Alec d'Urberville. She moved through the crowd to the door of the barn, her heart beating in suspense. Then she saw him, standing before the crowd in the afternoon sunlight.

Till this moment, she had never seen or heard from d'Urberville since her departure from Trantridge. His appearance had changed. The moustache was gone, and his clothes were more sober. For a moment Tess doubted that it was really him. Then there could be no doubt that her seducer stood before her.

There was something grotesque about solemn words of scripture coming out of that mouth. Less than four years earlier she had heard that voice use the same powers of persuasion for a very different purpose. Everything about him was transformed, and yet the difference was not great. The aggressive energy of his animal passions was now used for an equally aggressive religious fanaticism.

'But perhaps I am being unfair,' thought Tess. 'Wicked men do sometimes turn away from wickedness to save their souls.'

Just then Alec recognised her. The fire suddenly went out of him. His lips trembled. His eyes avoided hers. Tess hurried away from the barn.

As she walked away from the barn, her back seemed sensitive to eyes watching her, his eyes. She walked quickly, desperate to get as far away from him as possible. 'Bygones will never be bygones,' she thought bitterly, 'until I am a bygone myself.'

Then she heard his footsteps behind her. 'Leave me alone!' she cried.

'I deserve that. But, Tess, of all the people in the world, you - the woman I wronged so much - are the one I should try to save!'

'Have you saved yourself?' asked Tess with bitter irony.

'Heaven has saved me, and it can save you too!'

'How dare you talk to me like this, when you know what harm you've done me! I don't believe in your conversion or your religion!'

'Why not?'

Tess looked into his eyes and said slowly, 'Because a better man than you does not believe in it.'

'Don't look at me like that!' said Alec abruptly. His animal passions were subdued, but they were not dead.

'I beg your pardon,' said Tess, and she suddenly felt, as she had felt often before, that she was doing something wrong simply by inhabiting the body that Nature had given her.

He told her to cover her face with her veil. She did so, and they walked together as far as the intersection of the roads. On the way, she told him about the first of her troubles. He was shocked to hear what she had suffered. 'I knew nothing about it till now!' he said at last. Then they reached the intersection called Cross-in-Hand, where there was a stone pillar with the image of a human hand on it.

'You will see me again,' he said.

'No,' she answered. 'Don't come near me again!'

'I will think. But before we part, come here. Place your hand upon this pillar and swear that you will never tempt me.'

'How can you ask such a thing?'

'Do it.'

Tess, half-frightened, put her hand on the stone and swore.

They parted ways, and Tess went on alone towards Flintcomb-Ash. After a few minutes, she passed a solitary shepherd. 'What is the meaning of that stone pillar at Cross-in-Hand?' she asked. 'Was it ever a Holy Cross?'

'No! It is a thing of bad omen, Miss. It was put there in old times by the family of a criminal who was tortured there. They nailed his hand to a post and then they hanged him. His bones are buried beneath the pillar. They say he sold his soul to the devil, and that his ghost walks at night.'

A cold February wind blew across the dull brown field. Tess worked monotonously. She did not notice the figure approaching her. D'Urberville came up to her and said, 'I want to speak to you, Tess.'

'I told you not to come near me!' cried Tess.

'When we last met, I was concerned for the condition of your soul. I didn't ask you about your worldly condition. I see now that your life is difficult. Perhaps this is in part my fault.'

She did not reply but continued working as before.

'I want to recompense you for the suffering I have caused. My mother died recently, and The Slopes is now mine. I intend to sell the house and go to Africa as a missionary. Will you be my wife and go with me?'

'No!'

'Why not?' He sounded disappointed. He felt it was his duty to marry her, but it was also his desire.

'I have no affection for you. I love somebody else,' said Tess.

'Have you no sense of what is morally right?'

'Don't say that! Besides, I cannot marry you because I am married to him.'

'Ah!' he exclaimed. 'Who is your husband?'

'I won't tell you,' said Tess. 'No one here knows that I am married.'

'And where is he? Why is he not with you?'

'Because I told him about you.'

'He abandoned you?'

'Go away! For me and for my husband, go in the name of your own Christianity!'

Just then the farmer rode into the field. 'Get back to work!' he shouted angrily at Tess.

'Don't speak to her like that!' cried Alec.

'Go - I beg you!' said Tess.

'I can't leave you with that tyrant.'

'He won't hurt me. He's not in love with me.'

'All right,' said Alec reluctantly. 'Goodbye.'

When he was gone, Tess imagined herself married to Alec and all his wealth. 'But no,' she thought. 'I could never marry him: I dislike him so much.'

That night she wrote a letter to Clare. But then she remembered that he had asked Izz to go to Brazil. Perhaps he did not care for her at all. Instead of sending the letter, she put it in her box.

One day, when Tess was alone in her lodgings, Alec appeared at the door. He came in, sat down, and said, 'It's no use. I cannot resist my attraction to you. Ever since I saw you that Sunday, I have been thinking about you all the time. I was an enthusiastic convert, but now I have returned to my old way of thinking. Sometimes I think you are like Eve in Milton's Paradise Lost, and I am the serpent. You should pray for me Tess.'

'I cannot pray for you. I don't believe that God will alter his plans for me.'

Alec asked her about her beliefs, and she repeated things that Angel had said to her. They were arguments against the kind of religion preached by Angel's father, the same that Alec now preached. She remembered every word, although she did not understand it all. Alec listened thoughtfully to the arguments.

'Today I should be preaching at Casterbridge Fair, but instead I am here. Give me one kiss, Tess. Then I will go away.'

'No! I am a married woman! Leave me!'

'All right,' he said, and he did feel ashamed. Nevertheless, his religious sense of guilt had been weakened by the arguments that Tess had repeated to him. As he left the cottage, he said to himself, 'That clever fellow never thought that, by telling her those things, he might be helping me to get her back!'

Time passed and Alec's passion for Tess grew. He came to see her often. 'Be mine, Tess,' he often said to her. 'I'll give you all the money you want. I'll give you a life of ease.' But Tess refused.

In March, the farmer hired a threshing machine. He always gave Tess the hardest jobs. Now she had to stand on the back of the machine from dawn to dusk, in clouds of dust and noise, untying the sheaves and feeding corn into the machine. It was back-breaking work. Often she looked up and saw Alec, elegantly dressed, waiting for her by the hedge. He had stopped preaching now and stopped wearing the sober clothes of a religious man. In desperation, Tess wrote to Angel:

'My own HUSBAND - Let me call you so - even though I am an unworthy wife. I must cry to you in my trouble. I have no one else! I am so exposed to temptation, Angel. Please come home to me now, before something terrible happens. You are right to be angry with me. But please come to me, even if I do not deserve it. Angel, I live entirely for you. I love you. I don't blame you for going away. But I am so desolate

without you, my darling. Save me from what threatens me!

Your faithful heartbroken

TESS

Angel Clare looked out over the wide plain. He was sitting on the mule that had carried him from the interior of South America to the coast. His experiences of this strange land had been sad. He had been very ill shortly after arriving here and had never fully recovered. Now he had given up hope of starting a farm here. Many other farmers from England had suffered and died in Brazil. In twelve months Angel's mind had aged twelve years. He now valued the pathos of life more than its beauty. Now he saw that the true beauty or ugliness of a person lay in his intentions: his true history was not the things he had done but rather the things he had willed. Viewing Tess in this light, he regretted his judgement of her. His travelling companion on this last journey had been an Englishman who had lived in many different countries. They had talked together frequently and intimately. Eventually, Angel had told him about the sorrows of his marriage. To the other's cosmopolitan mind, Tess's deviation from the social norm was insignificant. He had said, 'What Tess had been is much less important than what she will become. I think you were wrong to leave her.'

Soon afterwards, the Englishman caught a fever and died. Clare began to feel remorse about his treatment of Tess. Izz's words were repeated over and over again in his mind: 'No one could love you more than Tess did!'

As he thought about these things, Tess's letter was travelling over the ocean towards him. She had sent it to his parents: that was the only address she had. They had forwarded it to him. But in the meantime, Tess was feeling sad and discouraged. She often thought, 'He will never return!' Then one clay in April her sister Liza-Lu came to Flintcomb-Ash. Liza-Lu had grown so tall and thin that Tess hardly recognised her at first.

'Is something wrong at home?' asked Tess.

'O Tess! Our parents are ill and we don't know what to do!' The poor girl began to cry.

Tess and Liza-Lu returned to Marlott that night. Soon after Jack Durbeyfield died. Her mother and the other children were all in deep distress because of her father's death. The next day, the owner of their cottage told them to leave by the end of the week. Now that Jack was dead, they had no right to stay there. Joan said they should go to Kingsbere, where the d'Urbervilles were buried. Tess agreed, though she knew that it was a foolish plan.

On their last evening in Marlott, Tess sat by the window, watching the rain outside. All their possessions were packed. Tess's mother and the children had gone to bed. Suddenly there was a knock on the door. When Tess opened it, she saw Alec standing outside in a white raincoat. 'Ah,' she said. 'I thought I heard a carriage.'

'I came on horseback,' said Alec. 'Perhaps you heard the d'Urberville coach. Do you know that legend?'

'No. Someone was going to tell me once, but he didn't.'

'It is rather depressing,' said Alec, coming in. 'If a d'Urberville hears the coach it is a bad omen. One of the family abducted a beautiful woman. She tried to escape from the coach in which he abducted her. In the struggle, he killed her, or she killed him - I forget which. I see you are all packed and ready to go.'

'Yes. Tomorrow we go to Kingsbere.'

'Listen, Tess,' said d'Urberville. 'Bring your family to The Slopes. The cottage that was once the chicken farm is empty now. I will have it cleaned and painted, and you can live there. I want to help you.'

'No,' said Tess.

'Damn it, Tess, don't be a fool. I shall expect you at The Slopes tomorrow.'

When he had gone, Tess took a pen and wrote the following letter: 'Oh why have you treated me so badly, Angel? I do not deserve it. I can never forgive you! You know that I did not intend to wrong you. You are cruel! I will try to forget you. T.'

'Who was your visitor last night, Tess?' asked her mother the next morning. 'Was it your husband?'

'No. My husband will never come.'

She had said that it was not her husband. Yet Tess was becoming more and more aware that in a physical sense this man alone was her husband.

When Tess and her family arrived at Kingsbere, they found the lodgings they had hooked were already taken. Tess and Liza-Lu ran through the streets, looking for other rooms, but none was free. They returned to the cart, where their mother and the children were waiting with all their boxes and furniture.

'Never mind!' said Joan. 'Unload everything here!' The cart was standing outside Kingsbere Church. 'I suppose your own family tombs are your own property? Then we will sleep in the churchyard!'

They carried the old four-poster bed into the churchyard and put it by the south wall of the church. Above it was a stained-glass window, in which they could see the d'Urberville emblems - the lion and castle familiar to them from their own seal and spoon. Joan drew the curtains around the bed and put the children inside. Then she and Liza-Lu went to find some food.

Tess went into the church. A figure lay upon one of the d'Urberville tombs. Suddenly Tess realised that this figure was not marble but a living man. It moved. The shock was so great that she nearly fainted. Alec jumped off the tomb and supported her. 'Tess, I - a sham d'Urberville - can do more for you than all these real ones. Now command me. What shall I do?'

'Go away!' she cried.

'All right. I'll go and find your mother. But you will be civil to me yet!'

When he had gone, she bent down on the entrance to the vaults below and whispered, 'Why am I on the wrong side of this door?'

CHAPTER TEN

Fulfillment

In May Angel Clare returned to England with two letters in his pocket. He went briefly to his parents at Emminster and then hired a gig and set out to find his wife. His parents were shocked to see how much he had changed. His face was thin, and his eyes were anxious. He wore a beard now, which made him look much older than he was.

Clare passed the stone pillar at Cross-in-Hand and went on to Flintcomb-Ash, to the address from which her letters had been sent. None of the villagers there could remember anyone called Mrs Clare: they had known Tess only by her Christian name. Clare found this discouraging. Her refusal to use his name, like her refusal to go to his father for help, showed a dignified sense of their total separation. And here for the first time Clare understood the hardships she had suffered in his absence. The farm workers told him that Tess had gone to her parents in Marlott, and so he continued his journey.

Clare's gig entered the lovely valley in which his dear Tess had been born and descended the green slopes to the village of Marlott. The villagers told him that Mr Durbeyfield was dead, and Mrs Durbeyfield and the children had left Marlott.

Clare began to despair. He went for a walk through the village to plan his next step. He passed by the field where Tess and the village women had danced all those years ago. He passed through the graveyard and saw John Durbeyfield's grave. On the gravestone were engraved these words:

John Durbeyfield, rightly d'Urberville, direct descendant of Sir Pagan d'Urberville, a knight of William the Conqueror. HOW THE MIGHTY ARE FALLEN

The people who now lived in the Durbeyfield's cottage gave Clare Joan's present address. He hired a gig and went there as fast as he could.

Clare had never met Joan before. When she answered the door, he noticed that she was a good-looking woman in respectable widow's dress. She looked at him nervously. He told her he was Tess's husband, and that he was looking for Tess. Joan was reluctant to give him the address. She said she was sure that Tess did not wish him to find her. But Clare did not believe her. He remembered Tess's first letter. 'Please tell me her address, Mrs Durbeyfield, in kindness to a sad and lonely man!'

Finally Joan told him that Tess was at Sandbourne - a fashionable seaside resort near Egdon Heath. Clare thanked her and hurried away to catch the next train for Sandbourne.

Joan had been unable to give Clare an address. All she knew was the name of the town in which Tess was now living. Clare walked down the fashionable streets of Sandbourne, looking at the shops and restaurants, he wondered what Tess - his young wife, a farm- girl - could be doing here. There were no cows to milk, no fields to harvest. He went to the post office and asked if they knew the address of Mrs Clare. The postman shook his head.

'Or Miss Durbeyfield?' asked Angel.

'No. But there is someone named d'Urberville at The Herons.'

The postman gave Clare directions to a small elegant hotel.

Clare rang the doorbell of The Herons. The proprietor - Mrs Brooks - answered the door and said, yes, there was a Mrs d'Urberville in the house. She asked Angel to wait in the sitting- room and went upstairs to call Tess.

'O dear!' thought Angel. 'What will she think of me? I have changed so much.'

Then he heard Tess's step on the stair, and his heart beat painfully.

Tess appeared at the door. She was not at all as he had expected. She wore a grey cashmere dressing gown. Her whole appearance was that of an elegant lady with plenty of money.

'Tess,' he said. 'Can you forgive me for going away?'

'It's too late,' Tess replied, her eyes shining unnaturally.

'I didn't understand, but now I do.'

'Too late! Too late!' she said, waving her hand impatiently like someone in great pain. 'Don't come close to me, Angel!'

'Don't you love me anymore? I know I look different. I've been ill. Please come with me.'

'I waited and waited for you!' she cried in her musical voice. 'But you did not come! He kept saying, "Your husband will never come back!" He helped my family. He won me back to him. Now I hate him, because he lied. You have come back! But it's too late!"

Angel stood still and silent for a minute when he heard this. Then he said, 'Ah! It is my fault!'

She ran upstairs. After a while he left the house.

Mrs Brooks had heard part of this conversation from her room, which was opposite the sitting room. Curious, she went upstairs and looked through the keyhole of the door to the d'Urbervilles' apartment. Through the keyhole she saw the breakfast things she had brought them earlier, and she saw Tess, lying on the floor, weeping. She heard Alec's voice ask, 'What's the matter?' Tess leapt up and replied with passionate fury. Afraid of being caught listening at the door, Mrs Brooks went downstairs quickly and quietly and sat in her room. All was now quiet in the d'Urbervilles' room above. After a while, she saw Tess leave the house.

Mrs Brooks rested her head on the back of her chair. Looking up, she noticed a spot the size of a wafer in the middle of the white ceiling. As she looked, the spot grew to the size of a hand. It was red. The rectangular white ceiling, with this red spot in the middle, looked like a gigantic heart.

Mrs Brooks ran upstairs and listened at the d'Urbervilles' door. The only sound was a regular beat: drip, drip, drip.

She opened the door, and there, on the bed, she saw Alec d'Urberville in a pool of blood with the bread-knife in his heart.

'Angel! Angel!' called Tess. Angel turned round and saw her running towards him. She was so pale and breathless that he took her hand and led her off the road into the forest. When they were hidden among the trees, he looked at her.

'I have killed him!' she said, and a pitiful white smile lit her face.

'What?'

'I never loved him at all as I love you! I thought you didn't love me anymore, so I went back to him. But now I have killed him, so say you love me, Angel!'

'I love you,' he said, holding her tightly in his arms. 'But have you really killed him?'

'Yes. I was crying after you left - my heart was breaking! He asked me why, and I became so furious I screamed at him. Then he ridiculed me for loving you, and he called you terrible names. And then I did it!'

He kissed her and said, 'I will not desert you! I will protect you, love, whatever you have done!'

At first, Clare did not believe that she had killed d'Urberville. Perhaps she had tried to kill him. Clare's horror at her impulse was mixed with amazement at the strength of her love for himself. Her love seemed to have extinguished her moral sense. Now that she was with Clare again, she seemed content. Nothing else seemed to matter. He looked at her face and thought of the d'Urberville coach. Perhaps the legend arose because the d'Urbervilles had been known to do these things.

They walked deeper into the forest. For miles and miles they walked, happy to be together alone at last. At noon they came to an inn. Angel told Tess to stay hidden among the trees. He entered the inn and returned with enough food for two days. They ate in the forest then walked on. Towards evening they came to a large house. It stood alone in the forest. On the gate was a sign saying, 'Furnished mansion for rent.'

'It is empty!' said Tess. 'We could spend the night here.'

Some of the windows were open. Tess and Angel climbed in through a ground-floor window. They went upstairs and into one of the bedrooms. It was a large room full of old-fashioned furniture. In the middle of it was a huge four-poster bed. Angel put down his bag and the package of food. He sat on the bed and said, 'Rest at last!'

As they ate, Tess told him about the night he carried her across the river and put her in the abbot's coffin.

'Why didn't you tell me the next day?' he asked.

'Don't think about the past,' she said. 'Just think of the present. Who knows what tomorrow will bring?'

The next day was cold and rainy. They stayed in the mansion all day and the next night. Angel went out and bought some more food at a shop some miles away. They stayed in the mansion for five days. They spoke of the past, but only the distant past, before their wedding day. On the fifth day, Clare said, 'We should leave this place.'

'Why?' asked Tess. 'We are so happy here. Inside this house is contentment. Outside is trouble.'

It was true. Inside was love, forgiveness, and peace. Outside was danger. 'I know, my love,' said Clare. 'But soon someone will come to clean the house. We must not be found here.'

The next day was sunny. They travelled north. Soon they came to the edge of the forest. They decided to sleep in the afternoon and continue their journey at night, under the cover of darkness. They passed through a silent sleeping town and on to the plain beyond. After walking for hours, they came upon a great stone structure.

'What is it?' asked Tess. It was made of enormous blocks of stone. Some stood erect, others were lying on the ground.

'It's Stonehenge!' said Clare.

'The pagan temple?'

'Yes. It is older than the centuries, older than the d'Urbervilles!'

Tess lay down on one of the stone slabs. 'I don't want to go any further,' she said.

Clare knelt down beside her. 'Are you tired? The stone you are lying on looks like an altar.'

'Angel, if anything happens to me, will you take care of Liza- Lu?'

'I will.'

'She is so good and simple and pure. Please marry her if you lose me.'

'If I lose you, I lose everything!'

Gradually the sky grew paler and the great blocks of stone stood dark against it.

'Did they sacrifice to God here?' asked Tess.

'No. I think they worshipped the sun.'

'Angel, do you believe we will meet again after death?'

He did not answer but kissed her instead.

'Oh! I fear that means no!' she cried with tears in her eyes.

She clasped his hand, but after a while he felt her grip relax in sleep.

The great plain was now visible in the morning light. The sun rose behind the Sun stone. Light bathed the Stone of Sacrifice. Clare saw something moving in the distance. He heard footsteps behind him. To his right and his left he saw men moving towards them. So her story was true! Clare leapt up and looked for a weapon.

'It's no use, sir,' said one of the men. There are sixteen of us.'

Tess woke up. 'What is it, Angel?' she asked. 'Have they come for me?'

'Yes, dearest.'

'I am almost glad,' she said. This happiness was too much. I have had enough.' Then she turned to the policeman and said, 'I am ready.'

On a warm July morning, Angel Clare and Liza-Lu climbed the hill above the city of Wintoncester. It was a fine old city, once the capital of Wessex County. Clare and his sister-in-law walked hand-in-hand, their heads bent with sorrow. She was taller and thinner than Tess, but she had the same eloquent eyes. When they reached the summit of the hill they looked out over the landscape and the Gothic spires of Wintoncester. The cathedral bells rang eight o'clock. Clare and Liza-Lu stared at the sound. They stared down at a large ugly building in the middle of the city. On one of the building's towers stood a flagpole. A few minutes after the hour had struck, something moved slowly up the flagpole. It was a black flag.

'Justice' was done. The President of the Immortals had ended his sport with Tess. The d'Urberville knights and ladies slept on in their tombs unawares. Clare and Liza-Lu knelt down on the ground as if in prayer. They remained there a long time. Then they rose, joined hands again, and went on.

- THE END -

Made in the USA
Middletown, DE
16 October 2023